The Fairy Berry Bake-Off

DISNEY FAIRIES

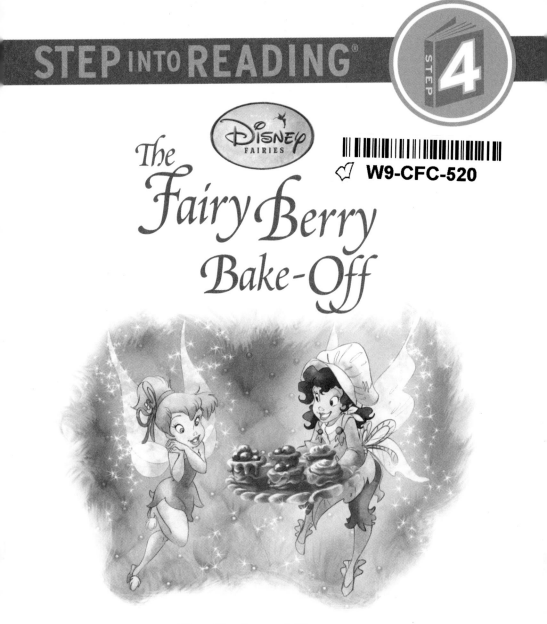

By Daisy Alberto

Illustrated by the Disney Storybook Artists

Random House 🏠 New York

All over Pixie Hollow, the Never fairies were hard at work. Each fairy had a talent and a special job to do.

The garden-talent fairy Lily was in her garden, watering the seedlings.

The art-talent fairy Bess was in her studio, working on a new painting.

The water-talent fairy Silvermist was collecting dewdrops.

The light-talent fairy Fira was training the fireflies to light Pixie Hollow at night.

The animal-talent fairy Beck was helping a lost baby chipmunk find his way home.

And Tinker Bell, a pots-and-pans fairy, was in her workshop, fixing a broken frying pan.

But no matter how busy they were, the fairies all stopped what they were doing at lunchtime. They headed to the tearoom to eat.

The tearoom was one of the most popular places in Pixie Hollow. It was peaceful. It was pretty. And best of all, the food was yummy!

The fairies gathered there every day for all of their meals.

"I wonder what tasty treats the baking-talent fairies will have for us today," said Lily.

"Maybe we'll have whole roasted cherries with cinnamon glaze," replied Bess.

"Yum!" exclaimed Tink. "I'm so hungry, I could eat a whole cherry all by myself."

The other fairies laughed. They couldn't wait to find out what was for lunch.

Strawberry soup, nutmeg pie,
blackberry cake, and roasted walnuts
stuffed with figs—every fairy had a
favorite dish!

There were so many wonderful treats, Tinker Bell couldn't decide what to try first. At that moment, something special caught her eye. She popped a tiny tart into her mouth.

"That's the best tart I've ever had!" she said.

In the kitchen, Dulcie, a baking-talent fairy, overheard Tink. "Tinker Bell loves my tarts!" she exclaimed with a smile.

Dulcie was proud of her baking. She always tried to make the fluffiest rolls, the flakiest pies, and the creamiest frosting. She really loved to bake. But she also loved to watch the other fairies enjoy her tasty treats.

The baking-talent fairy Ginger was nearby. When she heard Dulcie, she frowned.

"I think that was one of *my* tarts," she told Dulcie.

"Oh, I don't think so," Dulcie said sweetly. "Your tarts tend to be a little dry and hard."

Ginger most certainly did not agree. She knew that her tarts were always moist and flaky.

The next day, Dulcie baked
blueberries with fresh whipped
cream. The fairies ate every last one.

"Yum!" said Tink. "Are there
any more?"

Dulcie blushed. She beamed.

"They love my baking!" she said
proudly.

Dulcie wanted to be the best
baking-talent fairy in all of Pixie
Hollow.

Back in the kitchen, Dulcie peeked into the oven. She saw Ginger's gingerbread.

"It looks a little flat," she said. "You should follow my recipe, Ginger. My gingerbread is much fluffier."

Ginger had had enough of Dulcie's bragging.

"My gingerbread is perfect," she said.

"No, it isn't. But don't feel bad," said Dulcie. "Some fairies just need more practice than others."

That did it! Ginger was fed up.

"Dulcie, you wouldn't know what to do with a berry if it fell into your piecrust!" said Ginger.

"Ha!" said Dulcie. "I could outbake you any day!"

"Prove it," said Ginger.

"You're on!" cried Dulcie.

The fairy berry bake-off began. Ginger and Dulcie were going to prove once and for all who was the best baker. It was a battle neither fairy wanted to lose.

That evening, Ginger made boysenberry custard served in a vanilla bean. Dulcie made her magic blackberry turnovers.

"Wow!" said Tink. "They really
do turn over!"

The next day, Ginger made her famous five-berry crumble. The fairies cleaned their plates and licked every last crumb from their spoons.

Dulcie peeked into the tearoom. "Hmmph," she said. "Wait until they try *mine*."

Dulcie carried her right-side-up upside-down cake into the tearoom and proudly placed it on a table. The fairies didn't even notice. They were too busy finishing Ginger's five-berry crumble.

Dulcie couldn't believe it.

"Don't you like my cake?" she asked the fairies.

"It looks wonderful," said Tink. "But we're full."

Dulcie frowned. "How about just a little taste?" she pleaded.

The fairies shook their heads. They patted their stomachs.

"We couldn't eat another bite," Bess said.

Ginger grinned. It looked like
she had won this round of the berry
bake-off.

Dulcie knew she needed to make something extra-special for the next meal. So for lunch the following day, she outdid herself.

There were puddings and pies. There were crumpets and cakes. There were piles of Tink's favorite cream puffs.

The fairies ate and ate until they couldn't eat any more. Dulcie's feast was a hit.

But the berry bake-off was only getting started.

The next day at breakfast, Dulcie and Ginger waited in the tearoom for the fairies to arrive.

"Try a muffin," Dulcie said to Tink. "They are soft and sweet."

"How about a honey bun?" asked
Ginger. "They're even softer and
sweeter."

"No, a muffin!" said Dulcie.

"A bun!" cried Ginger.

"Er, I'm not hungry," said Tink,
flying away.

Dulcie and Ginger didn't even
notice that Tink had left.
They kept arguing.

The fairies worked hard all
morning. They were looking forward
to a nice, relaxing lunch. Dulcie and
Ginger met them as they entered the
tearoom.

Dulcie waved a spoon. "Taste this!" she called out.

"No, taste this!" shouted Ginger. "Mine's better!"

But none of the fairies stopped. The tearoom no longer seemed very relaxing at all!

Back in the kitchen, things were no better.

"Get me an egg!" Dulcie shouted to an egg-collecting fairy.

"I need more flour!" Ginger snapped at a kitchen-talent sparrow man.

One by one, the other fairies left
the kitchen. They didn't want to be
around Dulcie and Ginger. The berry
bake-off was getting out of control.

Soon Dulcie and Ginger were
alone in the kitchen. But they didn't
notice. They were both too busy.

They sifted and stirred. They
mixed and measured. They each
wanted their next dessert
to be their best.

Ginger made fresh raspberry cupcakes with vanilla cream filling. She used the finest raspberries that grew in Pixie Hollow.

Dulcie made her special seven-layer cake, with six kinds of berries.

Dulcie reached for a berry to top off her cake.

"That's *my* berry!" Ginger exclaimed. "You can't have it."

"It's *my* berry," Dulcie replied. "I'm sure of it."

"It's mine!" said Ginger. She
grabbed the berry.

"No, it's mine!" said Dulcie. She
held on tight.

Neither fairy wanted to give in.
They pulled and pulled, until . . .

. . . Dulcie stumbled backward—
right into her cake!

Ginger stumbled backward, too.
Her cupcakes went flying
everywhere!

"Oops!" said both fairies at once.

One cupcake hit Dulcie. Another hit Ginger.

Just then, Tink walked in to see what all the fuss was about. A flying cupcake landed right on her head.

"Hey!" cried Tink. "What is going on here?"

Dulcie and Ginger looked around. The kitchen was a disaster. Cake and cupcakes were everywhere!

"Oh, no!" said Dulcie.

"What have we done?" cried Ginger.

They rushed over to Tink.

Tink was mad. "The berry bake-off has gone too far," she said. "Don't you understand that you are both great bakers?"

Dulcie and Ginger blushed. They looked at each other. Could it be true? Could they *both* be great bakers?

Dulcie brushed Ginger's cupcake crumbs off her apron. She tasted her fingers.

"Oh, my," said Dulcie. "This is good!"

"Really?" asked Ginger.

"Yes!" said Dulcie.

Ginger smiled. She took a tiny taste of Dulcie's seven-layer cake.

"Wow," she said. "So is yours!"

"Why don't you bake together?" Tink suggested.

And so the fairy berry bake-off
ended in a tasty tie.

To my sweet boys,
Jack and Nathan.
—D.A.

Step into Reading, Random House, and the Random House colophon are registered trademarks of Random House, Inc.

Visit us on the Web!
www.stepintoreading.com
www.randomhouse.com/kids/disney

Educators and librarians, for a variety of teaching tools, visit us at
www.randomhouse.com/teachers

Library of Congress Cataloging-in-Publication Data
Alberto, Daisy.
The fairy berry bake-off / by Daisy Alberto. — 1st ed.
    p. cm. — (Step into reading)
Summary: Ginger and Dulcie have a bake-off to see who is the best baking-talent fairy in Pixie Hollow.
ISBN 978-0-7364-2525-4 (trade pbk.) — ISBN 978-0-7364-8061-1 (lib. bdg.)
[1. Fairies—Fiction. 2. Baking—Fiction. 3. Competition (Psychology)—Fiction.] I. Title.
PZ7.A3217Fai 2008
[Fic]—dc22
2007029196

Printed in the United States of America   10 9 8 7 6 5 4   First Edition

Dear Parent:

Congratulations! Your child is taking the first steps on an exciting journey. The destination? Independent reading!

STEP INTO READING® will help your child get there. The program offers five steps to reading success. Each step includes fun stories and colorful art. There are also Step into Reading Sticker Books, Step into Reading Math Readers, Step into Reading Write-In Readers, Step into Reading Phonics Readers, and Step into Reading Phonics First Steps! Boxed Sets—a complete literacy program with something for every child.

Learning to Read, Step by Step!

Ready to Read Preschool–Kindergarten
• big type and easy words • rhyme and rhythm • picture clues
For children who know the alphabet and are eager to begin reading.

Reading with Help Preschool–Grade 1
• basic vocabulary • short sentences • simple stories
For children who recognize familiar words and sound out new words with help.

Reading on Your Own Grades 1–3
• engaging characters • easy-to-follow plots • popular topics
For children who are ready to read on their own.

Reading Paragraphs Grades 2–3
• challenging vocabulary • short paragraphs • exciting stories
For newly independent readers who read simple sentences with confidence.

Ready for Chapters Grades 2–4
• chapters • longer paragraphs • full-color art
For children who want to take the plunge into chapter books but still like colorful pictures.

STEP INTO READING® is designed to give every child a successful reading experience. The grade levels are only guides. Children can progress through the steps at their own speed, developing confidence in their reading, no matter what their grade.

Remember, a lifetime love of reading starts with a single step!